Dear Parent:

Congratulations! Your child is taking the first steps on an exciting journey. The destination? Independent reading!

STEP INTO READING® will help your child get there. The program offers five steps to reading success. Each step includes fun stories and colorful art. There are also Step into Reading Sticker Books, Step into Reading Math Readers, Step into Reading Write-In Readers, Step into Reading Phonics Readers, and Step into Reading Phonics First Steps! Boxed Sets—a complete literacy program with something for every child.

Learning to Read, Step by Step!

Ready to Read   Preschool–Kindergarten
• big type and easy words • rhyme and rhythm • picture clues
For children who know the alphabet and are eager to begin reading.

Reading with Help   Preschool–Grade 1
• basic vocabulary • short sentences • simple stories
For children who recognize familiar words and sound out new words with help.

Reading on Your Own   Grades 1–3
• engaging characters • easy-to-follow plots • popular topics
For children who are ready to read on their own.

Reading Paragraphs   Grades 2–3
• challenging vocabulary • short paragraphs • exciting stories
For newly independent readers who read simple sentences with confidence.

Ready for Chapters   Grades 2–4
• chapters • longer paragraphs • full-color art
For children who want to take the plunge into chapter books but still like colorful pictures.

STEP INTO READING® is designed to give every child a successful reading experience. The grade levels are only guides. Children can progress through the steps at their own speed, developing confidence in their reading, no matter what their grade.

Remember, a lifetime love of reading starts with a single step!

For Lilly Grace—M.L.

Step into Reading, Random House, and the Random House colophon are registered trademarks of Random House, Inc.

Visit us on the Web!
www.stepintoreading.com
www.randomhouse.com/kids
Educators and librarians, for a variety of teaching tools, visit us at
www.randomhouse.com/teachers

Library of Congress Cataloging-in-Publication Data
Lagonegro, Melissa.
Tink's treasure hunt / by Melissa Lagonegro; illustrated by the Disney Storybook Artists. — 1st ed.
p. cm. — (Step into reading. Step 3)
ISBN 978-0-7364-2612-1 (trade) — ISBN 978-0-7364-8072-7 (lib. bdg.)
I. Disney Storybook Artists. II. Tinker Bell (Motion picture) III. Title.
PZ7.L14317Ti 2009 [E]—dc22 2009006112

Printed in the United States of America 10 9 8

STEP INTO READING®
STEP 3

Disney fairies

TinkerBell
AND THE
LOST TREASURE

Tink's Treasure Hunt

By Melissa Lagonegro
Illustrated by Denise Shimabukuro, Jeff Clark,
Merry Clingen, Adrienne Brown, Charles Pickens,
and the Disney Storybook Artists

Random House 🏠 New York

The fairies of Pixie Hollow
are bringing autumn
to the mainland.
Leaves change color.
Pumpkins ripen.
Birds fly south
for the winter.

4

In Pixie Hollow,
the dust-keeper fairies pack
and deliver pixie dust.
Fairies need pixie dust
to fly and to make magic.

After work,
Terence visits Tinker Bell.
She is building a boat.

Tink takes her boat for a ride.
She speeds through the water.
"Oh, no!" she cries.
Her boat crashes!
Luckily, she isn't hurt.

Then Queen Clarion
calls Tink to her chamber.
The Minister of Autumn is there.

He tells Queen Clarion,
Fairy Mary, and Tink
about the Autumn Revelry.

Every year, the fairies create
a special autumn scepter.
This year, it's Tink's turn
to make it!

She must build the scepter
with a very rare moonstone.
The blue harvest moon's rays
will pass through the moonstone.
It will create blue pixie dust
for the Pixie Dust Tree!

Terence helps Tink.

Tink molds metal.

Terence keeps the fire burning.

The two fairies make a great team.

They work together
day and night.
Tink sets the moonstone.
It is very heavy.
Terence gives Tink advice.

"Steady," he says.
Tink gets annoyed.
A piece breaks off the setting.
Terence goes to find
a tool to fix it.

Finally, Tink finishes
the scepter.
Terence returns with a compass.
He thinks its parts
will fix the broken setting.
But Tink is still annoyed.
She pushes the compass
out of the way.

The compass rolls
into the scepter.
The scepter breaks into pieces!
Tink is angry with Terence.

Tink tells Terence to leave.
Then she kicks the compass.
It smashes into the moonstone!
Tink is very upset.

Clank and Bobble visit Tink.
They invite her to
the Fairy-Tale Theater.
She agrees to go.

The show is about
the Mirror of Incanta.
The mirror can grant one wish.
But it was lost in a shipwreck
on a faraway island.
Tink wants to find the mirror!
She wants to use the wish.
She wants to fix
the broken moonstone.

Tink draws a map
of the faraway island.
She makes a list.
She gathers supplies
and checks the compass.
She has a plan!

Tink builds a balloon.
She uses cotton balls
and a gourd.
She works very hard.

The balloon is finished.

Tink hops in.

She flies away from Pixie Hollow.

It is late. Tink is hungry.
But her food is gone!
A firefly named Blaze
ate it all.

Blaze shines his light.
Now Tink can read her map.
Blaze can help Tink
on her trip!

Soon Tink finds the island.

She sets out to explore.

Blaze stays with the balloon.

The balloon breaks loose.

Blaze tries to warn Tink.

But it is too late.
Tink's balloon floats away.
Now her supplies are gone!

Tink is hungry.

Blaze calls for his friends.

They bring honey and water.

Then they show Tink the way.

Back in Pixie Hollow,
Terence goes to Tink's house.
He finds moonstone pieces,
the list, and the
balloon drawing.
Tink needs his help!
He goes to find her.

Tink and Blaze sneak
past two trolls.
Tink knows
the mirror
can't be far!

They find the shipwreck!
"This is it!" Tink cries.
She must go inside
to find the mirror
and fix the moonstone.

Tink and Blaze go into
the dark and spooky ship.
Blaze lights the way.

They find the mirror!

"I wish . . . ," Tink begins.

But Blaze buzzes in her ear.

She tries again.

Blaze buzzes some more.

"Blaze, I wish you'd be quiet!"

Tink yells.

Blaze stops buzzing. Oh, no!
Tink used her one wish!
Her eyes fill with tears.
"I wish Terence were here,"
she cries.
Then she sees him
in the mirror.

Terence found Tink.

He is on the ship!

Tink is so happy to see him.

The two friends hug.

Just then,
rats surround them!
Blaze pretends to be a monster.
He makes a big shadow.
The rats are scared.
They run away.
"Let's go," says Terence.

They find the balloon!
Tink has an idea.
She and Terence can fix
the scepter with the
moonstone pieces.
They work together.
Blaze helps.

Back in Pixie Hollow,
the Autumn Revelry begins.
Tink presents the scepter.
The moonstone is in pieces.
But moonbeams reflect
off each piece.
Blue pixie dust rains down.
There is more blue dust
than ever before!

This Autumn Revelry
is the best one ever!
Everyone thanks Tink
and her very special friends.